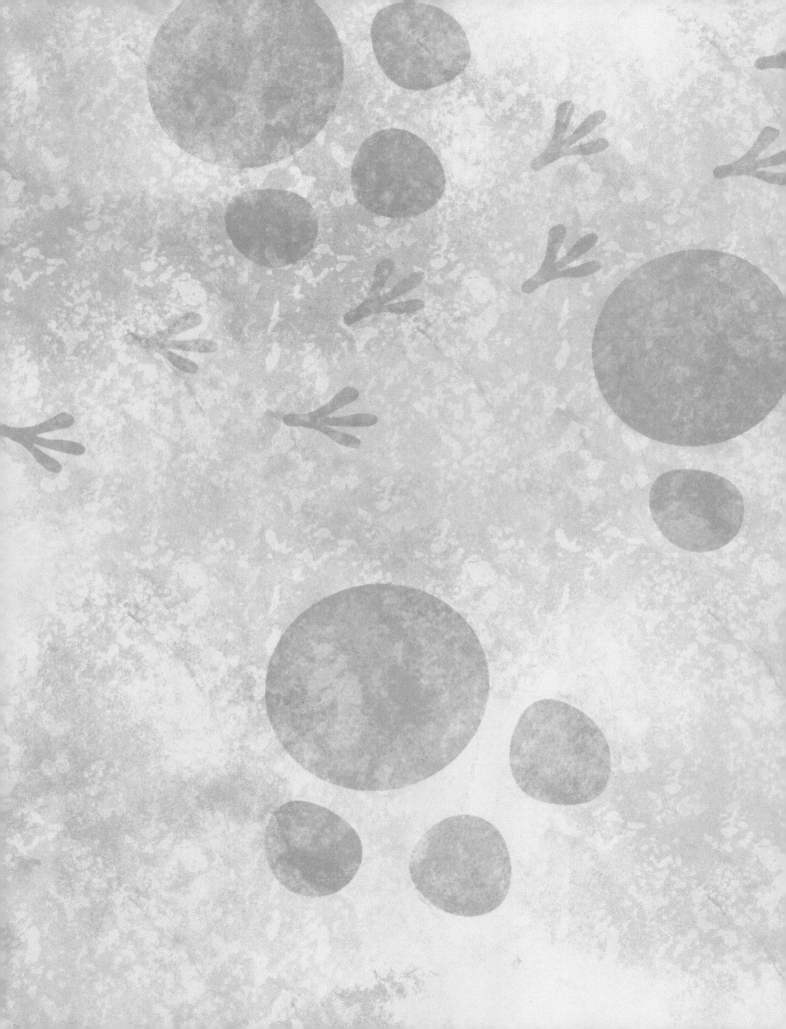

Marley
The Street Cat

Written
by
Sharron Taylor

Illustrations
Picasso Griffiths

Marley the street cat,
Lived by the deep blue sea.
On the Greek island of Kefalonia,
In a village called Sami.

His days were filled with lazing
Like a lizard in the sun.
His nights were full of adventure,
As he roamed about looking for
some fun!

Marley had no family,
He spent all his time alone.
He also had no friends,
And no place to call his home.

He often slept in the bushes,
And ate his dinner from the bin.
He would hide away from the
other cats,
Who liked to chase him!

Every day he wandered hungrily,
Around the tavernas along the dock.
Hoping to find a tasty snack to eat,
Or a fresh fish, if he was in luck!

He always meowed politely,
And rubbed gently against their legs.
He waited very patiently,
And tried so hard not to beg.

Some people were very kind,
And would spare him some food.
Others shooed him away,
As they found him rather rude!

Sometimes he went hungry,
Other days he ate like a King!
But Marley was still so tiny,
And he was very, very thin!

He was also very smelly,
And covered in lots of bugs.
Nobody wanted to stroke him,
Or give him any hugs.

He tried so hard to make friends,
With the other street cats on the bay.
But they would just stick out
their tongues,
And quickly run away!

Marley was very sad and lonely,
All he wanted was a friend.
Someone special that he could love,
And all his time he could spend.

Often people didn't stop to pet him,
Even when he began to cry.
They just held their noses tightly,
And quickly hurried by!

Until one day a nice lady,
Saw him sitting alone on the path.
She picked him up gently,
And took him home for a bath!

She spoke to him softly,
And tickled him gently under his chin.
She filled his tummy with delicious food,
And smiled as he rubbed against her skin!

She took him for a visit to the vet,
Who got rid of all his bugs.
She let him fall asleep on her lap,
And gave him lots of hugs!

She put him on a soft warm bed,
With some toys on a mat.
Then locked him safely in a cage,
With another cat!

Her name was Lucy,
She didn't want to run away.
She rolled on her back,
And just wanted to play!

Marley felt so happy,
That he let out a loud "Purrrrrr!"
He curled up in a sleepy ball,
As his new friend groom his fur!

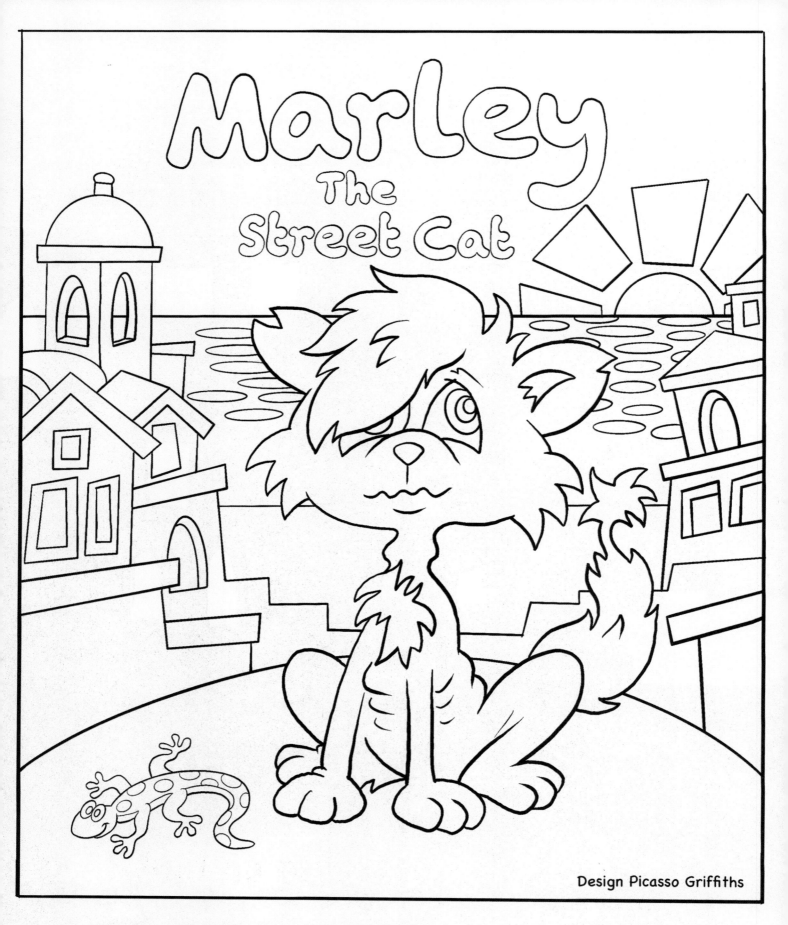

Marley Poster Colouring Page

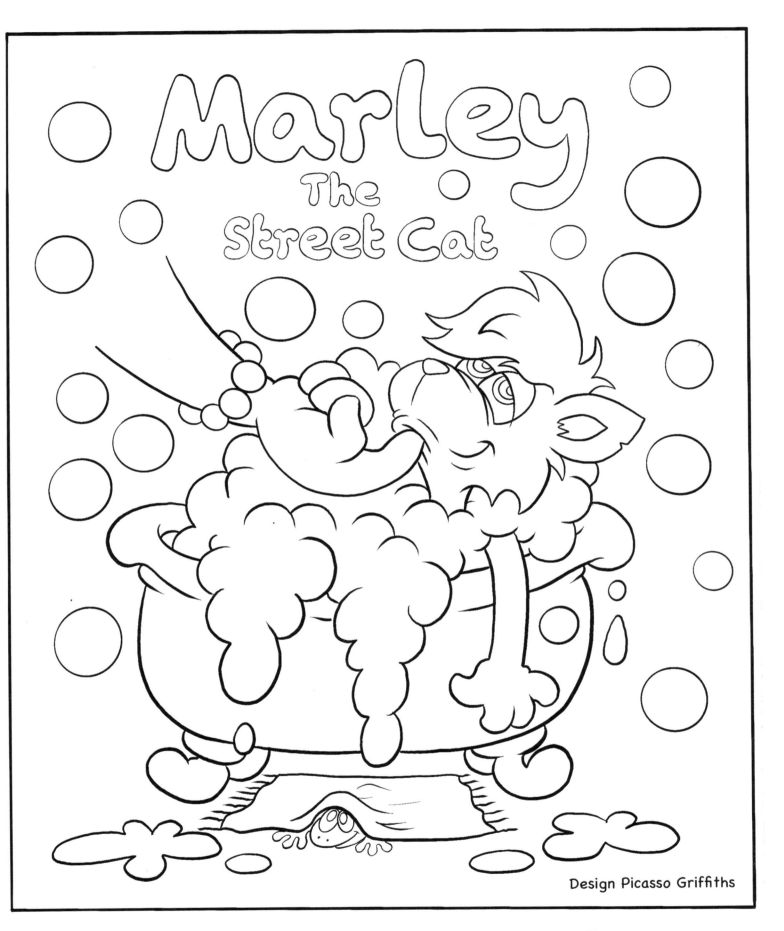

Marley Poster Colouring Page

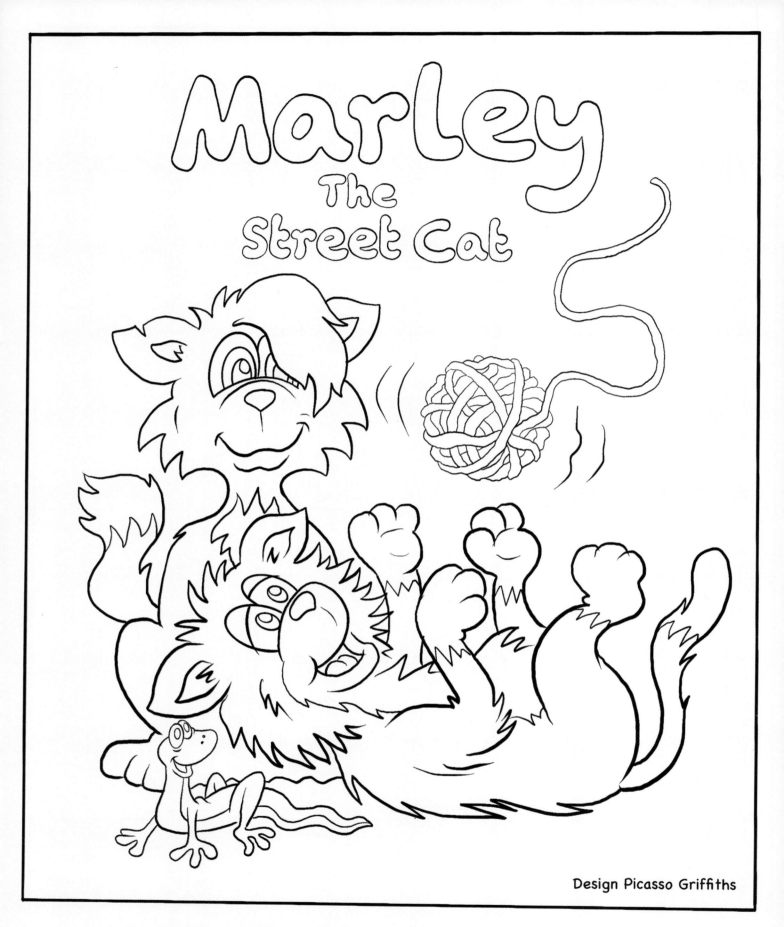

Marley Poster Colouring Page

Have a go at drawing a street cat

Printed in Great Britain
by Amazon